MICKEY MOUSE CLUBHOUSE

Mickey is the leader of the Clubhouse gang. He is great at getting his friends excited for an adventure. Mickey is happiest when he is exploring or learning something new with his Clubhouse friends by his side.

Minnie is Mickey's best gal pal. Whether she's planning the perfect picnic, primping pets at the pet salon, or going on a Clubhouse adventure, Minnie is up to the task. Her friends can always count on her for a creative solution to any problem.

Pluto is Mickey's dog and best friend. He loves playing fetch and burying bones in the Clubhouse yard.

Donald has a big heart, a loud squawk, and a lot of energy. When Donald sets his mind to something, he is determined to make it happen, no matter what challenges come his way—but he usually needs a little help from his friends. His fits of frustration are balanced out by his fits of laughter.

Daisy is Minnie's best friend and Donald's sweetheart. Daisy will do anything for her friends. Even though she sometimes loses her temper, Daisy is always ready to help anyone in need.

Goofy is kind to everyone who crosses his path. Just like his name, Goofy can be a goofball! He is sometimes forgetful but always remembers to be a good and caring friend.

Are We There Yet?

Written by Sheila Sweeny Higginson and
adapted by Joanna Green
Illustrated by the Disney Storybook Art Team
Designed by Elizabeth Andaluz

Disney PRESS

It is a beautiful day at the Clubhouse.
"Let's go to the beach," says Daisy.
"Everyone hop in the car!"
says Mickey.
"I know the way," says Donald.

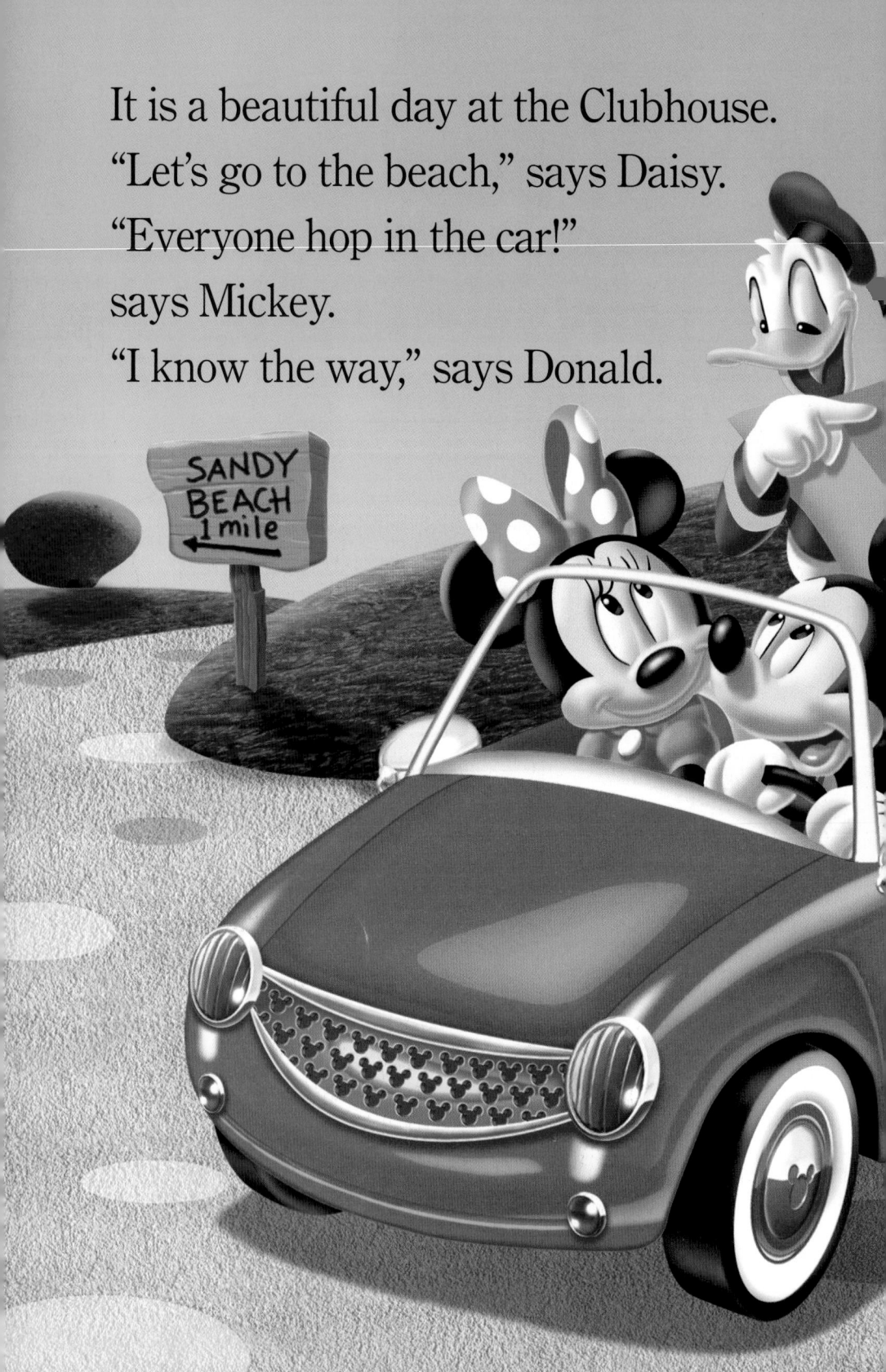

SANDY
BEACH
1 mile

They drive and drive.
"Are we there yet?" Mickey asks.

This place is very hot.
There is a tall cactus.
This is not the beach.

It is the desert!
"Turn that way," says Donald.

They drive and drive.
"Are we there yet?" Daisy asks.

This place has many trees.
There are colorful animals.
This is not the beach.

It is the rain forest!
"The beach must be this way,"
Donald says.

Welcome
to the
RAIN FOREST

They drive and drive.
"Are we there yet?" Goofy asks.

This place is very cold.
There are penguins and seals.
This is not the beach.

It is Antarctica!
"The beach has be that way,"
Donald says.

Welcome to ANTARCTICA

They drive and drive.
"Are we there yet? asks Minnie.

This place is very green.
There are deer and rabbits.
This is not the beach.

It is the forest!
"I think the beach is to the
right," says Donald.
But everyone else points left.
They drive and drive.

Welcome
to the
CooL FOREST

"Are we there yet?" Daisy asks.
This place is sunny.

There is sand.
There are crabs and sea stars.

There is water.
There are dolphins and whales.

"We're here!" everyone cheers.

LESSON

A good friend helps you get to where you want to go.

Adapted by Lisa Ann Marsoli

Based on the episode written by Ashley Mendoza

Illustrated by Loter, Inc.

Disney PRESS

Mickey wants to surprise Minnie.
He needs to keep Minnie busy.
"Can you take care of my frog?"
Goofy asks.

"And sweep the floor?" Daisy adds.
"And wash my rubber duckies?"
says Donald.

"I have a lot to do," says Minnie.
First she washes the rubber duckies.

Next she fixes Pluto's bear.
"I'm so tired," says Minnie.
Soon she is asleep!

"Minnie-rella!" a voice calls.
"I'm your fairy godmother! It's time
to get ready for Prince Mickey's ball!"
Minnie-rella has too much to do.

The Fairy Godmother will help.
She waves her wand.
Oops! Flowers grow out of the floor!
"Oh, Quoodles," she calls.

Quoodles brings a pillow, a hippo, a ribbon, and the mystery tool. They will save the tools for later.

The Handy Helpers help clean.
"Now you can go to Prince Mickey's ball,"
the Fairy Godmother says.

"I need a dress," says Minnie-rella.
"Here," the Fairy Godmother says.
Oh, no! The dress is in pieces!
"Oops!" says the Fairy Godmother.

The Fairy Godmother whistles.
Some little friends come to help.
Soon Minnie-rella has a lovely dress.

Now Minnie-rella needs a new bow.
"Hmmm," says the Fairy Godmother.
"Which tool can we use?"
"The ribbon!" says Minnie-rella.

The Fairy Godmother looks down.
"Your shoes won't do at all!" she cries.

She waves her
wand once.

"Oops!"

She tries again.

"Oops!"

"Once more," says
the Fairy Godmother.

"That's it!"

"You're ready!" says the Fairy Godmother.
"How will I get there?" asks Minnie-rella.
They go to Goofy's garden.

The Fairy Godmother asks for a pumpkin.
"I don't have any pumpkins," Goofy says.
"But I've got a big tomato."

The tomato turns into a carriage.
Goofy turns into a coachman!
"Be home before midnight!"
says the Fairy Godmother.

On the way to the ball, the carriage gets stuck in a hole!

Minnie-rella calls Quoodles. Which tool can help?

Maybe the hippo can push the
carriage out of the hole!
The hippo taps the carriage.
Away it goes!

Soon Minnie-rella and Goofy come
to the castle gate.
"It takes three diamonds to unlock
the gate," Pete says.

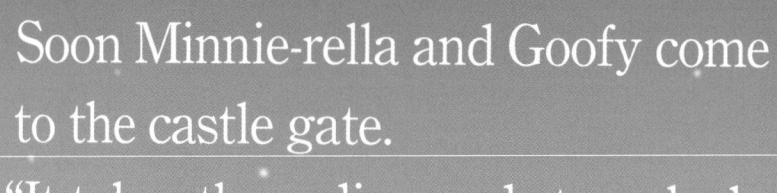

Quoodles brings the mystery tool.
It is a bracelet with three diamonds.
The three diamonds unlock the gate.
Minnie-rella can go to the ball!

Minnie-rella runs to the ball.
She dances with Prince Mickey.
Prince Mickey has found his princess!

Soon it is midnight.

"I have to go!" cries Minnie-rella.

"Wait! I don't know your name,"
  Prince Mickey calls.

"How will I find her?" he asks.
Pluto sees the glass slipper.
Prince Mickey must find the one
who fits the glass slipper.

Prince Mickey begins his search.
Goofy tries on the glass slipper.
It does not fit.

The slipper is going to break!
Quoodles brings the pillow.
Prince Mickey catches the slipper!

Goofy takes him to see Minnie-rella. The glass slipper fits!

The prince and princess will live happily ever after!

"Wake up, Minnie!" call her friends.
Mickey gives her a present.
"I dreamed of shoes like these!"
Minnie says. "Thank you!"

"You look like a princess,"
says Mickey.
"You'll always be my prince!"
Minnie says.

The friends do the Hot Dog Dance.
Minnie loves her new glass slippers.
She does the best dance of all!

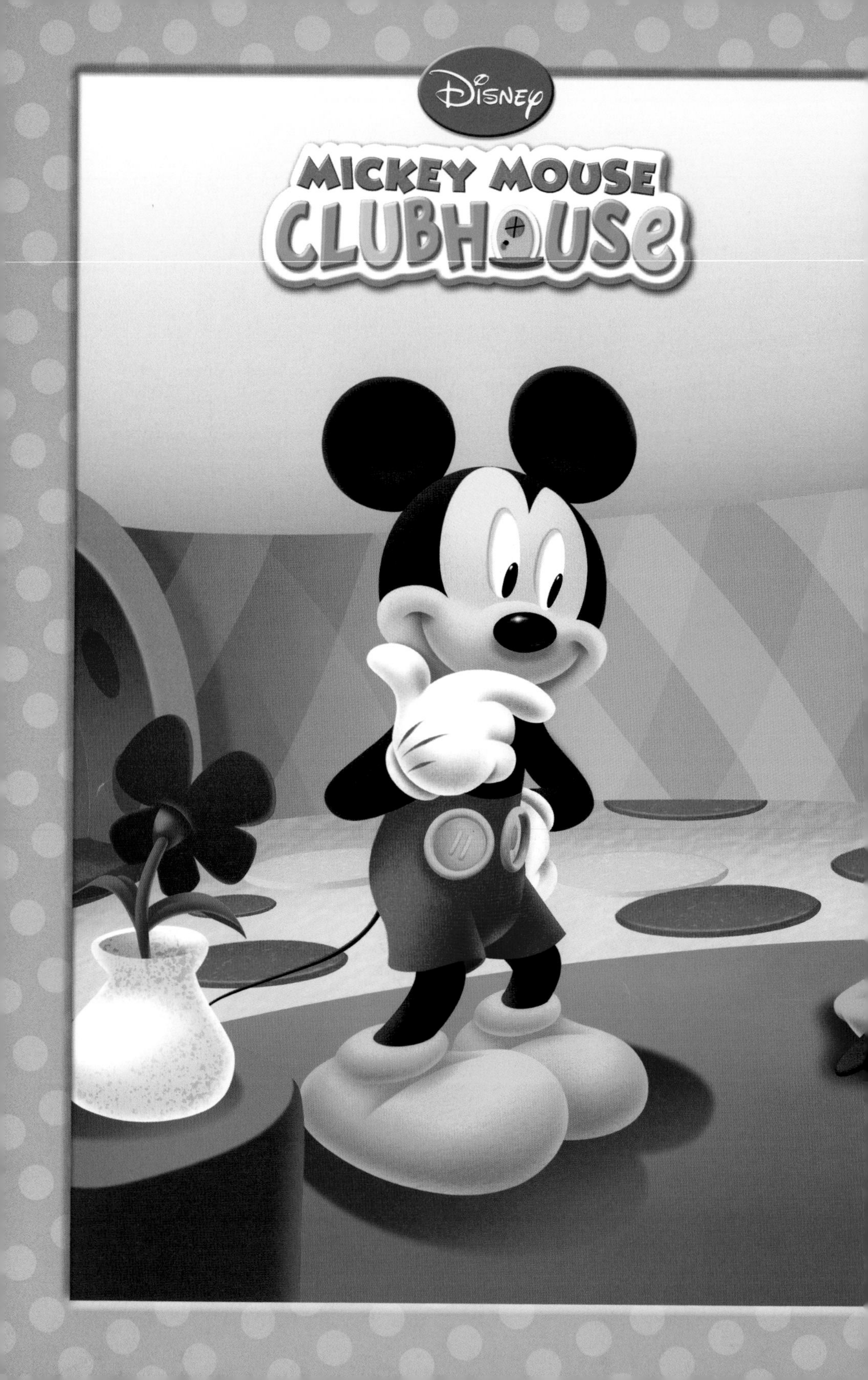
Disney
MICKEY MOUSE
CLUBHOUSE

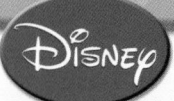

LESSON Good friends give each other good surprises.

Disney MINNIE'S PET SALON

Based on the story by Don Gillies & Ashley Mendoza
and on the episode written by Ashley Mendoza
Adapted by Bill Scollon
Illustrated by Loter, Inc.

DISNEP PRESS

Today is Pluto's Pet Show!
One pet will win a prize.

Minnie sets up a pet salon.
She will get all the pets ready.

Goofy wants his kitty to look good.
"And my frog, too!" he says.
Daisy brings her bunny!

Clarabelle gives Bella to Minnie.
Pete drops off his dog, Butch.
Donald brings Boo-Boo Chicken!

"So many pets!" says Minnie.
Minnie needs help.
Daisy and Donald will help.
So will Mickey and Goofy.

Daisy helps at the pet wash.
It is time for Bella's bath.
Daisy pours in the soap.
The bubbles grow and grow!

The bubbles cover Bella.
Daisy jumps in to find her.
"Help!" says Daisy.
Minnie comes running.

"Oh, Toodles!" calls Minnie.

Toodles brings the tools.

"The baby elephant will wash away
the bubbles," says Minnie.

The elephant sprays water.
The bubbles go away!
"Bella is ready for the show!"
says Daisy.

Donald wants to put bows
on the kitties.
"Sit still!" he says.

Minnie comes to help.
"We need a soft blanket," she says.
Donald calls, "Oh, Toodles!"

Toodles has three tools left.
One is soft like a blanket.
It is the towel!

The kitties jump into Donald's arms.
"It worked!" says Minnie.

The kitties get bows.
They are ready for the pet show!

Minnie goes to see Mickey.
He wants two pets to jump rope.
"They won't jump together," Mickey
says.

"This might help," says Minnie.
"One, two, jump when we do.
Three, four, jump once more!"
It helps! The pets jump together.

Butch and Bella run by.
"Slow down!" calls Goofy.
Goofy needs help.
"Oh, Toodles!" calls Mickey.

Mickey picks the Mystery Tool.
It is a big sock!

Butch and Bella stop running.
They play with the sock.

It's time for Pluto's Pet Show!
Pete and Clarabelle sit together.
They will pick the best pet.
Goofy turns on the lights.

"Gawrsh!" says Goofy.
"The lights aren't working!"
The show cannot go on.

Mickey calls, "Oh, Toodles!"

The last tool is the jar of fireflies.
The fireflies can light the show!
Super cheers!

Pluto barks.
"Now we can start the show!"
Mickey says.

Boo-Boo Chicken comes on first.
He does a chicken dance!

Butch and Bella are next.
They spin and dance!

The kitties jump through hoops.
Goofy and Minnie cheer!

The frog and the bunny
jump together.
Look at them go!

The friends are proud of their pets. Now Pete and Clarabelle must pick the best.

Clarabelle and Pete cannot choose.
They ask Minnie for help.

"I know!" says Minnie.
"All of our pets win!"

Everyone agrees.
The pets share the prize!

Mickey has a prize just for Pluto.
"You put on the best pet show ever,"
he says. "Hot dog!"

LESSON

Every pet deserves to be treated like a winner.